OLIVER &
AMANDA
AND THE BIG SNOW

Jean Van Leeuwen
PICTURES BY
ANN SCHWENINGER

DIAL BOOKS FOR YOUNG READERS

NEW YORK

To David and Elizabeth,
with fond memories of sledding,
snowmen, and snow forts

J. V. L.

For Donna Peck

A. S.

Published by
Dial Books for Young Readers
A Division of Penguin Books USA Inc.
375 Hudson Street
New York, New York 10014

The Dial Easy-to-Read logo is a registered trademark of
Dial Books for Young Readers,
a division of Penguin Books USA Inc., ® TM 1,162,718.

Library of Congress Cataloging in Publication Data
Van Leeuwen, Jean.
Oliver and Amanda and the big snow
Jean Van Leeuwen; pictures by Ann Schweninger.—1st ed.
p.   cm.
Summary: Four stories about Amanda and Oliver Pig and their
parents, who go outside to play after a big snowstorm.
ISBN 0-8037-1762-8 (trade).—ISBN 0-8037-1763-6 (library)
[1. Snow—Fiction. 2. Brothers and sisters—Fiction.
3. Family life—Fiction. 4. Pigs—Fiction.]
I. Schweninger, Ann, ill. II. Title.
PZ7.V327301i 1995 [E]—dc20 93-48598 CIP AC

First Edition
1 3 5 7 9 10 8 6 4 2

The full-color artwork was prepared using carbon pencil,
colored pencils, and watercolor washes. It was then scanner-separated and
reproduced as red, blue, yellow, and black halftones.

Reading Level 1.7

CONTENTS

DIGGING OUT

It snowed all day.

It snowed all night.

"Look at all that snow!" said Oliver.

Amanda looked out her window.

She could not see anything.

"Even your window is covered
with snow," said Mother.
Amanda looked out the door.

Everything everywhere was white.
"It is the biggest snow I ever saw,"
she said.

"Let's go outside," said Oliver.

"You will have to dress warm,"

said Mother.

She dressed them in a lot of sweaters

and snowsuits and scarves

and woolly hats and mittens.

"I am so warm that I can't move,"

said Amanda.

Outside, everything looked different.

The apple tree was a crooked ghost.

The bushes were fat scoops
of ice cream.

The bird feeder wore a white hat.

And Oliver's fort had disappeared.

"Where did it go?" asked Oliver.

"It was right there," said Amanda.

She went looking for it.

Suddenly she disappeared too.

"Where is Amanda?" asked Oliver.

"Down here," came a tiny voice.

Father fished her out of a snowdrift.

"This snow is deep," he said.

"You better stay with me."

Father shoveled.

Oliver and Amanda made footprints.

They threw snowballs.

They found long, shiny icicles.

"This is my magic sword," said Oliver.

"With it I am Captain Brave."

"This is my magic wand," said Amanda.

"With it I can turn snowflakes

into butterflies."

Amanda waved her wand
and disappeared.

"Wow!" said Oliver. "It *is* magic."
"Help!" squeaked a tiny voice.
Father dug her out of a snowbank.
"How about helping me shovel?"
he asked.

Scrape went three shovels.

Crunch went the snow.

When they finished shoveling,
they had made a pile of snow
even taller than Father.

Oliver and Amanda climbed to the top.

"This is my new fort," said Oliver.

"We can make a hundred snowballs

and throw them at the bad guys.

Right, Amanda?"

"Right," said a tiny voice far away.

"Uh-oh," said Oliver. "She's gone again."

Father found her at the bottom

of the snow pile.

"I'm cold," said Amanda.

Father lifted her onto his shoulders.

"Let's go inside and get warm,"

he said.

Inside, Mother was waiting
with hot chocolate and cookies
fresh from the oven.

"How was the snow?" she asked.

"I like it," said Amanda.

"But it is a little too big."

THE SNOW FORT

Oliver was sitting on the snow pile

making a hundred snowballs.

Amanda was helping.

"I like my new fort," said Oliver.

"But it would be even better

if it had an inside.

I could keep my snowballs there

and we could hide from the bad guys."

"Let's do it," said Amanda.

"It's my fort," said Oliver.

"I want to do it myself.

You keep making snowballs."

Oliver started to dig.

"I made twenty-seven snowballs,"
said Amanda. "Now can I help?"
"No," said Oliver.
"We need a hundred."

He kept digging.
"I made forty-two snowballs,"
said Amanda. "And I'm not making
any more. Now can I dig?"
"I told you," said Oliver. "It's my fort
and I want to do it myself."

"Fine," said Amanda. "See if I care.

I am going inside."

"This snow is as big as a mountain,"

said Oliver.

But he kept on digging.

Amanda came outside with Mother.

They made snow angels.

They played the magic wand game.

Then Mother said, "Shall we try out

our sleds on the big hill?"

"Mother!" called Oliver.

"Would you help me dig?"

"We will be happy to," said Mother.

She and Amanda started on

the other side of the snow pile.

"If we dig from both sides," she said,

"we will meet in the middle."

Oliver kept digging

until he made a tunnel.

He heard Mother calling.

"Amanda, can you see Oliver yet?"

"No," said Amanda's voice.

"Oliver, can you see Amanda?"

"I see a red mitten," called Oliver.

"I see a blue mitten," said Amanda.

Oliver and Amanda shook mittens.

"We did it!" said Oliver.

They piled all the snowballs inside.

Oliver made a flag out of his hat

and a stick.

"Now we are ready for the bad guys,"

he said.

Just then a snowball hit the flag.

"They're here!" he said.

Snowballs went flying.

Soon the flag was knocked down,

and Oliver and Amanda

were almost out of snowballs.

"I give up," said a voice.

"It's not the bad guys," said Amanda.

"It's a polar bear. No, it's Father!"

"Your fort is great, Oliver,"

said Father.

Oliver put his flag back on top.

"You mean *our* fort," he said.

Amanda smiled.

And she and Oliver shook mittens.

SLEDDING

"Watch this!" called Oliver.

He went zooming down the big hill

on his little sled.

"I don't like this hill," said Amanda.

"It's too steep."

"We could try that little hill instead," said Mother.

"All right," said Amanda.

Amanda and Mother went slowly down the little hill on their big sled.

"That was nice," said Amanda.

"Watch this!" called Oliver.

He went whizzing backward

down the big hill on his little sled.

"Let's do it again," said Amanda.

This time they went a little faster.

"Watch this!" called Oliver.

He went spinning like a top

down the big hill on his flying saucer.

"I want to try it alone," said Amanda.

Mother gave her a push.

Amanda went all by herself

down the little hill on her big sled.

"Watch this!" called Oliver.

He spun around upside down,

backward, and no-hands

down the big hill on his flying saucer.

But his saucer bounced on a bump,

and Oliver went flying.

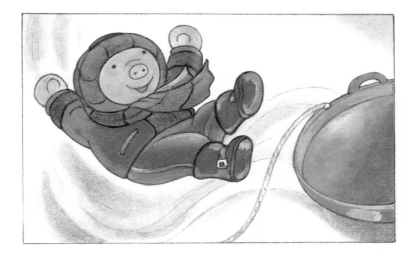

He picked himself up.

"That was fun!" he said.

"Come on, Amanda.

Let's make a sandwich."

"What is that?" asked Amanda.

"That is when we all ride together,"

said Oliver. "Mother on the bottom,

then you, then me.

See, you are the peanut butter

and we are the bread."

"All right," said Amanda.

"But only on the little hill."

They piled onto the sled.

Oliver gave a big push,

and jumped on top of Amanda.

"Ooof!" said Amanda.

They started down.

Faster and faster they went.

Amanda could not see anything.

She was squashed like peanut butter.

Then she felt a great big bump.

Suddenly she and Oliver and Mother

were all flying through the air.

"Are you all right?" asked Mother.

Amanda sat up.

Her hat was gone.

Her jacket was full of snow.

Her boots and mittens were full of snow.

She was up to her ears in snow.

"That was fun!" she said.

"Let's do it again—on the big hill."

They did it again.

And again. And again.

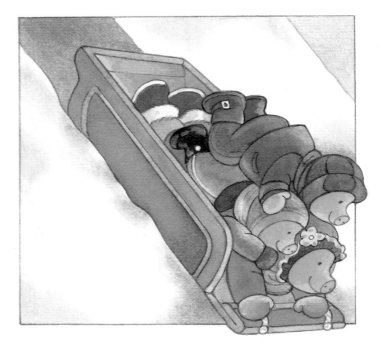

"Are you ready to go inside

and get warm now?" asked Mother.

"No," said Amanda.

"Now I want to do tricks."

So she and Oliver went zooming
and whizzing and spinning like tops
down the big hill.

THE SNOW PIG

"Look at my icicle," said Amanda.

"It keeps getting littler and littler."

"That is because the snow is melting,"

said Father.

"And that is the very best time

to build a snow pig."

"Hooray!" said Oliver and Amanda.

"First we will need three

very big snowballs," said Father.

He made a snowball.

Then he began to roll it.

The snowball grew bigger and bigger.

"I want to do one," said Oliver.

"Me too," said Amanda.

They began to roll snowballs.

"This is hard work," puffed Oliver.

"I'm done."

Father piled Oliver's snowball
on top of his.

"That is not very big
for its stomach," said Amanda.

Father piled Amanda's snowball
on top of Oliver's.

"That is not very round
for its head," said Oliver.

41

"I think our snow pig looks
just fine," said Mother.
"I am going to find it a hat and scarf."
"I will find it some eyes," said Father.

Oliver looked at the snow pig.

"It needs arms," he said.

He and Amanda rolled two arms.

Oliver put his on.

"Oh, no!" said Amanda.

"Its head fell off."

Oliver put it back.

43

"It is all crooked," said Amanda.

She put her arm on.

"Oops," she said. "It broke.

Oh well, it can be ears instead.

Look at my funny nose!"

"And my funny tail!" said Oliver.

When Mother and Father came back,
they asked, "What happened?"

"Hmmm," said Oliver.

"It doesn't look exactly like a pig."

"Maybe it is a monster," said Amanda.

"Or a motorcycle," said Father.

"Or an elephant," said Mother,

"standing on its head."

"Or a snorp," said Oliver.

"A snorp?" said Amanda. "What is that?"

"I don't know," said Oliver.

"I just made it up."

"I like it," said Amanda.

Every morning they looked

out the window at their snorp.

It got smaller.

"Now it looks like a castle,"

said Amanda.

"Or a crocodile," said Oliver.

And smaller.

Until finally it just looked like

a snowball sitting in the grass.

Oliver looked up at the sky.

"Uh-oh," he said.

"It is snowing again."

"Good," said Amanda.

"I hope it will be another big snow."